For Your Eyes Only

WORDS OF FAITH, LOVE & ROMANCE

LANETTA R. ALLEN

Because There's More Publishing | Georgia

ISBN: 979-8-9990652-2-3 (Hardback)
ISBN: 979-8-9990652-3-0 (Paperback)

Library of Congress Control Number: 2025911665

Printed in the United States of America.

Published by:
Because There's More Publishing LLC
PO Box 390163
Snellville, GA 30039
becausetheresmorepublishing.com

Dedication

To all those who have suffered a severe blow to the heart and wondered, "Will it ever be possible for me to love again? To trust again?" Yes, my sister. Yes, my brother. With God, anything is possible!

Acknowledgments

A special thank you to my Lord and Savior, Jesus Christ, for awakening me to the possibility of true love. God knew it would require an exercise in faith to embrace love again, and He gave me exactly what I needed - wholeness and the faith to love. Also, a special thank you to my family and friends, who always support and encourage me in my work.

Contents

FOR YOUR EYES ONLY

Prologue

SLEEPING BEAUTY:
THE UN-FAIRY TALE

I realize now that the only heart that has never been broken, hurt, disappointed, or wounded - is the heart that has never loved.

Many of us are familiar with the movie *Sleeping Beauty* - the tale of a beautiful princess lulled into a deep sleep after pricking her finger on a spindle, awakened only by the power of true love.

Only in the world of make-believe, right?

Not quite.

Sleeping Beauties still exist today - women and men who find themselves asleep to love due to deep wounds of the heart. And the "spindle" that caused their injury? Often, it's the hurtful words and actions of others.

Many of us know what it feels like to suffer a broken heart - disappointment, betrayal, pain. But what sets a Sleeping Beauty apart is that his or her heart becomes closed to the idea of ever embracing love again.

Do you know a Sleeping Beauty?

I was one of them.

I didn't want to open my heart to anyone again. Looking through wounded lenses, love seemed to carry risks I wasn't willing to take or become vulnerable to. So, I closed my heart and fell asleep to the very idea of love.

But like in the fairy tale, that wasn't the end of my story.

God has a way of surrounding us with people who love us through those broken places. Their love shows up in prayers, encouragement, listening ears, and wise counsel - people who genuinely have our best interests at heart.

Still, even Sleeping Beauty needed more than the good fairies' support to awaken. Her true awakening came when she was touched by the kiss of Pure Love - love expressed by the prince.

That became my story too. It took Pure Love - the love of my Prince of Peace. God's comforting words and the truth of His love awakened me from my emotional slumber.

As I once shared in a Facebook post: *The only heart that has never been broken, hurt, disappointed, or wounded - is the heart that has never loved.* That doesn't mean every relationship ends in heartbreak; it simply means heartache is a part of the human experience. You are not alone.

Even so, when you've experienced deep heartache, it can take extra grace and healing to find the faith to love again. Love does carry a risk - but for me, I would rather love than never have loved at all.

God healed and made my heart whole, so I could be free - free to love, and to receive the love of the prince He has for me.

Writing these pieces was a refreshing journey. It gave me an outlet to express the hopeful romantic in me - hopeful that true love is real, not just an abstract fantasy found in fairy tales or ancient truths in biblical narratives. There is a Ruth for Boaz, a Prince Charming for Cinderella, and yes, a Sleeping Beauty awakening to the kiss of Pure Love.

So, I invite you to join me as we explore the thrill of love's awakening - the fears and longings, the cautionary flags, and the faith to move beyond past pain and fully embrace love and romance once again.

Some of my personal desires and experiences are interwoven into these pages. Others were sparked through observation or through quiet moments of reflection with God.

Before you can
move forward in
love, sometimes
God must first
reintroduce you
to you -
not the version
marred by pain,
disappointment,
or expectation,
but the one He
originally
designed.

To My Son: Let Me Introduce You to You

It's been a long time, I know -
Since you've seen the real you.

Arriving on the scene
Looking all clean
Fitting the part
They just can't believe -
It's him…the Black king.

That smile
Those eyes
Those lips

Ooo…wish he was mine, the ladies say...
He's a real man.
The perfect man.

But what they don't realize -
it's partly a lie, a façade…
You lost the real you a long time ago.

The image overshadowed the person.
"I had to uphold it at all costs," you said to
yourself.

"This is what success looks like.
I'm on top of the world..."

Looking in the mirror at a reflection
you now don't recognize.
Trying to reimagine the real you -
the last time you saw you.

They marvel.
You weep.

For what you see is a cookie-cutter form,
not the original man God created and purposed you
to be.

You were made in the image and likeness of God.
But instead of conforming to His image
you conformed to theirs...

Look this way
Dress this way
Speak this way
Connect this way
Go to this school
Get this degree
Pursue this career
Make that money
Date this type of woman

Drive this type of car
Live in this type of neighborhood
Buy this type of house
Attend this church
Do it this way…

All this way, just to lose your way -

God!
Reintroduce me to me.

[God's Voice]
Son, take a seat and listen -
as I speak these truths to you.
As you have asked, so shall I do.

I remember the moment I met you -
a thought in My mind.

I immediately loved you.
You were the apple of My eye.
My thoughts towards you were
always good, not evil -
plans to prosper and see you to a successful end.

I had purpose for you in the earth.
So, I used your mother and father to conceive you
and I released you at the appointed time.

They were your birth parents
but you were always Mine.

I remember the first time
you held your mother's hand –
a gentle, yet strong grip.

She had to pry your little fingers
from around her thumb.
You were tenacious, even then.

When you set your eyes on something -
watch out –
there was no stopping you.

You were this rambunctious baby boy
with no fear.

And I saw you grow up into this
 inquisitive, creative adolescent.
Gifted hands, beautiful mind –
Art meets Einstein.

Didn't always fit.
Too peculiar for some.
But you embraced it head-on.

At that age - you were headstrong.

You refused to be defined or confined by
someone's opinion of you.
I created you to reflect Me!
Even then, you understood –
   you are bigger than the box!

I saw you grow into a secure young man!
Sure of your value
Sure of your masculinity
Sure of your identity!

I watched you pursue your dreams
with fervor and intensity –
Focused, determined, with a no-quit attitude.

Your light was so bright!
You are so bright!

Full of life.
Full of dreams.
Full of hopes.
Uniquely you!

The little boy that thought he could
Grew into the man that did!

But there are times
when the world can make you think -

That who you are is not enough
That you're not good enough.
So you set out to prove you are
and in the midst of the pursuit -
Forget who you are.

So, let Me introduce you to you!

You are My son.
You are enough.
You are good enough!

To My Daughter: You are Woman

Once upon a time
There lived a little girl -
Full of hope,
Full of dreams,
Excited about thc possibilities that life would
bring.

Free and carefree,
Loving unconditionally.

Then life happened…
Things unplanned,
Things unexplained,
Things that shook the very foundation
of who she was
- or thought herself to be.

Things that caused her to question
her very identity.
Things that caused her to doubt,
caused her to act out.
Things that made her cry…

Although you would never know -
She rarely let it show.

She wore her mask well:
The smile,
The laugh,
The talks,
The service,
The faithfulness,
The success.

Who you have known…

She didn't look like struggle.
Didn't see any visible wounds or battle scars.
She was mother, wife, sister, daughter, aunt,
friend, pastor, leader, co-worker, teacher…
Making it happen, doing what needed to be done.

Didn't see the resistance that came
to weaken her resolve.
The opposition that came to crush her hope.
The inner turmoil and the desire to violently break
free -
The naked eye couldn't see,
and she dare not say.

She remained silent,
without the victory she sought -
because she was afraid.

Afraid to confront the pain.
Afraid that saying it would somehow bring shame
or make her appear weak.
Not understanding…
She's not alone.

We have all struggled at some point,
With something - or some things -
including you and me.

She wasn't an oddity or abnormality -
as the enemy or her inner me
tried to make her think.

The opposite is true -
She is normal.
She is normal…

Now comes a sigh of relief.

Sounds funny to some,
as they think this is inherently known.
But many have suffered in silence
and lived a life bound -
because they did not know.

Her picture as a little girl
didn't include the conflict,

Tests and trials...
She only saw the happily ever after.

She didn't realize that everybody
wouldn't be for her -
That some would even dare to mistreat, violate,
and/or abuse her.

She didn't foresee the internal conflicts:
Jealousies, insecurities, complacency, and low
self-esteem -
or the external injustices of the various isms of our
society.

She didn't know she'd be faced
with an unseen enemy -
on her journey to destiny.

But God - who always knew -
had already made a way for her to overcome this
too.

What was meant to destroy her,
God would use to build her.

What was sent to disrupt and frustrate her,
God would use to develop and mature her.

What came to undermine her faith,
God used to teach her how to fight the good fight
of faith.

Now she understands.
Now she knows…

This is her epiphany:
*The trauma of my past didn't stop God's plan for
me.*
Nor does the struggle of my present
exempt me from experiencing God's best for me.

His thoughts for me are still good -
To give me a hope, a future,
an expected end in Him.
And peace…

She no longer has to hide from her past
or wear the all-too-familiar mask.

She can be free.
She can be free.
She can be free.

Free to share her story and fulfill her destiny.
Free to become the woman
 the little girl saw in her dreams.

The bold,
beautiful woman
who overcomes
and is able to encourage others
with her testimony.

Full of hope,
Full of dreams,
Excited about the possibilities that life will bring.
Free and carefree,
Loving unconditionally.

Who is she?

She is you –
and me.

Woman.

Wherever God's road leads you - be free...

I Am Free...Free to Love

There was a time when I wasn't free. Falling in love, to me, meant being vulnerable - vulnerable to the risk of being severely hurt again. After surviving a destructive marriage marked by abuse and infidelity, I had no desire to open myself up to that kind of heartache ever again. I would have much rather lived alone than lived with someone who was hurting me.

I became so content in my singleness that I even questioned whether it was God's will for me to marry. Maybe I was meant to be like the Apostle Paul - devoted solely to Christ.

It was easy for me to love God because I knew He loved me and had my best interest at heart. With Him, I didn't have to worry about being mistreated, taken advantage of, devalued, neglected, or ridiculed. At my worst, I experienced His love in a way that was real and tangible. I found peace and safety in His presence - and the strength I needed to break free from a very bad situation. God had proven Himself faithful and unconditional in His love for me. When you're loved like that, it's easy to love in return.

But the issue wasn't my ability to love God. It was my openness to love someone else, intimately again. Whether or not it was God's will for me to marry wasn't the core issue. What God was after was the motive behind my willingness to remain single: **fear**.

As God healed and made me whole - perfecting me in His love - the fear began to fade. I became open to the idea of marriage again. Now, I have a desire to share the whole woman I've become. To share this overwhelming love that fills my heart with the man God has purposed for me. That was a seven-year journey.

Does this mean I'm no longer content in my singleness? Not at all. More years have passed since then, and I am still very much in love with God. He is, and always will be, my first love. His love is the reason I can love myself and others.

It's important to understand that my desire for a spouse does not diminish my desire for God. The two can and do coexist. For whatever reason, some of us have compartmentalized the two, as if they can't share the same vessel. But I can be single, saved, and still desire to be an entrepreneur, to own a home, and more. The desire for a spouse shouldn't be viewed any differently.

It almost seems like some singles are afraid to publicly express their longing for marriage, as if doing so implies discontent with God. Sometimes that fear is valid - but often, it's not.

Now, let me say this: there are those whom God has indeed called to a life of celibacy. This is not the same as abstinence, which is the practice of refraining from premarital sex (as all unmarried persons are called to do). Celibacy is a vow to remain unmarried and abstinent for life. The conclusion of my seven-year journey could very well have ended with that calling and I would have embraced it with peace.

For me, the freedom to love didn't begin with the hope of a wedding day. It started when I chose to open myself fully to God's love and yield completely to His timing. And in that surrender, I trust that, when the time is right, that same freedom will flow into the heart of the one He's preparing for me.

Free to Be

I am,
You are.

Forgiven.
Redeemed.
Exonerated.
Emancipated from our past -
We are FREE.

Yes! Free indeed, for the Son has set us free!

Free to be who God created us to be:
His royalty.
His prince and princess.
Yes - sons and daughters of the King.

Becoming.
Evolving.
Transforming.
Morphing into the
Man,
Woman,
God is calling forth in you and me.

The world no longer sways us -

We rest in God's definition of "we."
Yes, that's true liberty.
True freedom.
True security.

We're FREE to be...

My heart has been revived and awakened to love.

Springtime, My Love is Here

Hear the birds singing -
Making melody in their hearts.

Hear the wind whistling
As it moves effortlcssly across the landscape,
Soft breezes cooling the heat of the sun.

Hear the trees clapping -
For refreshing has come.

Hear the flowers rejoicing -
Their set time has arrived.
That which was dormant is now:
Budding,
Opening,
Blossoming,
Blooming.
Thanking God -
For they have been revived.

Hear the people shouting praises to God:
The joy of the Lord is our strength!
The joy of the Lord is our strength!
As they bask in the newness of His Presence
And the sufficiency of His Grace.

Don't you hear?
Springtime is here.
Yes, springtime is here...
And look -
my Love is riding on her wings,
heading straight for me!

Put a little pep in your step,
a little glide in your stride -
and ride the tide -
the tide of joy, that is.

It's springtime, and My Love is Here!

**Love always
blooms in the
spring.**

The Moment I Saw You

I remember when I first really saw you.
You'd always been there,
working in ministry,
doing what God has called you to do.
But I never truly saw you...
until that moment.

It wasn't your looks that gained my attention -
Though you are a beautiful man.
It wasn't the way you walk or talk.
It wasn't your piercing eyes
or that infatuating smile
that made me take note of you...
to really see you.

It was your prayer for others.
I know... it sounds corny, but it's true.

For a season,
it just so happened that when
you would minister in prayer -
I'd be nearby.
And I noticed -
Your genuineness,
Your deep concern for each person.

To see a man minister in love and sincerity -
it was beautiful.
To hear and see you minister through prayer -
blessed me.

It's not that others didn't do the same,
but in that moment...
I saw you.

And then the day arrived -
you ministered to me.

To have a godly man embrace me
and earnestly pray for me
was refreshing.

There were no hidden motives.
No sexual overtones -
Just true,
real,
compassion.

I thanked God for you.

It was the spiritual you.
The God in you -
that caused me to really see you...
in that moment.

The Giver.
Divine Intervention

The Gift.
Knowing My Worth

The Receiver.
Recognition and Readiness

I Am A Gift

The Word says, "He who finds a wife finds a good thing and obtains favor from the Lord" (Proverbs 18:22). If I may paraphrase: he who receives a wife receives benefits and obtains favor from the Lord.

Some people say that God doesn't choose our spouse for us, but I disagree. I believe that God directs us toward His perfect will, but it's up to us to heed and follow His direction.

I take the Word as written:
"The steps of a good man are ordered by the Lord"
(Psalm 37:23), and
"Trust in the Lord with all your heart and lean not on your own understanding; in ALL your ways acknowledge Him, and He shall direct your paths"
(Proverbs 3:5–6).

That being said, God has given us free will - the ability to choose to accept or reject His leading.

I've said to God what many other women have voiced or at least thought:
"God, I want to be pursued! I want a man who is not just interested in the outside covering, but is

willing to open the book and thoroughly read it. I don't need some superficial brother... I want a fully grown man, who knows what he wants and isn't afraid to pursue - pursue me!"

But then God said something that made me rethink that idea of "pursue me."

He said:
"I am a Gift.
Gifts are received, not pursued.
The order is to pursue Me, and I'll give the Gift."

That shifted my perspective.

The danger in only focusing on the pursuit is that some men are addicted to the thrill of the chase. He wants to handle the gift - touch the gift - play around with the gift, without investing the time and commitment required to fully unwrap the gift.

But understand your position:
You are a Gift.

If he wants you, he must receive you as My Gift –
and then unwrap you.

Too many women unwrap themselves in hopes of gaining the affection of a man I never intended to be the recipient of the gift.
A gift never unwraps itself.
That's the responsibility of the receiver.

And when the receiver understands the value of the gift, the more carefully he unwraps it - and the more dearly he holds what has been given to him.

You are a Gift.
A Gift with Benefits and Favor from God.

Let him make inquiry of Me concerning you.
Let him seek ways to open you up and discover the treasures within.
Let him search for ways to please you and to sow into you -

Until he fully unwraps and obtains the benefits and favor that come from receiving the Gift...
as his wife.

My sisters, let me hear you say:
"I am a Gift."

RE: I Am A Gift

I never said, "You weren't a gift."
Woman of God, I know your value -
I know that you are God-sent.

You assumed I didn't recognize you,
solely based upon my response to you.
But did you ever consider, my dear,
that the issue wasn't a matter of desire -
But God's timing in receiving you?

A real man won't unwrap prematurely.
He'll keep passion under control
until he's truly ready to commit.

So don't count me out.
When God says, "IT'S TIME,"
Believe me -
there will be no hesitation on my part.

I look forward to:
Receiving,
Unwrapping,
Discovering,
Loving,
Spending a lifetime exploring God's Gift to me.

Danger Zones
CAUTIONARY FLAGS

> Above all else, guard your heart, for everything you flows from it.
> *Proverbs 4:23 NIV*

Warning is defined as:

[1]A statement or event that indicates a possible or impending danger, problem, or other unpleasant situation.

You may ask, "Why include a warning section in a book about faith, love, and romance?"

The answer is simple: to offer some cautionary advice as it relates to relationships and matters of the heart.

This short interlude focuses on three potential danger zones:

1. Excess Baggage
2. Premature Love
3. Greener Grass Mentality

Most of us desire to know love, be loved, and to love. But in our eagerness, we may enter relationships with unresolved issues (Excess Baggage), move too fast (Premature Love), or assume that what's on the outside is better than what we currently have (Greener Grass Mentality). Each

---

[1] Dictionary.com

of these can have detrimental effects on both the heart and the relationship.

1. Excess Baggage

For example, there was excess baggage I needed to deal with in my own life so I could present a whole person to the prince God has for me. I didn't want to be like a coffee mug full of holes - leaking out whatever was poured in. I wanted not only to give love, but also to receive it and be able to hold love.

Now, I'm not saying you have to be perfect to move forward in a relationship. But you do need to be honest with yourself about any unresolved issues. The danger of excess baggage is that it can cloud our view of a person and place undue strain on a new relationship.

The Little Foxes gives us insight into the small things that can destroy when left unresolved.

2. Premature Love

Another danger zone is what I call Premature Love - love stirred up before both parties are ready to enter a committed relationship. One person may want more than the other is ready or willing to give.

Most of us want to be with the right person, but sometimes we overlook the more important question:

"God, is this the right time?"

Suddenly, we find ourselves emotionally attached and in love with someone who isn't prepared to reciprocate. If ignored, this can deeply wound the heart. So if God says, "Wait" - wait!

The Other Forbidden Fruit warns us of the danger of premature love.

Bonus Reflection: ***Wolf in Sheep's Clothing***

This reflection reminds us to look beyond appearances and charisma to discern a person's true nature. Everything that shines isn't gold, and everything that looks good isn't necessarily good for you.

Watch and pray!

3. Greener Grass Mentality

The danger of this mentality is the illusion that something (or someone) else is better - when in reality, it is not. From a distance, almost anything can appear appealing. But as you get closer, the truth reveals itself and you realize it wasn't greener after all.

By then, you may want to go back... but sometimes it's too late.

The Girlfriend on the Inside reflects that regret.

Though this reflection is written from a married person's perspective, there's a powerful lesson for singles too:

Don't miss out on God's best, looking for "better."

The man in this story went looking for more when - he already had God's best in his wife. Let this be a reminder: you can never do better than God's best.

We must continue to seed, water, and nurture our relationships so they remain fresh, vibrant, and green (to play on the phrase). If you think a relationship requires no effort to grow, you're sadly mistaken. God may divinely connect, but we are responsible for maintaining what He joins together.

A Note for My Sisters

The Girlfriend on the Inside also sends a strong message to us as women.

The woman in this reflection lost a sense of who she was in her marriage. Her self-worth became marred by insecurities - sometimes perpetuated by an abusive spouse and other times by comparing herself to other women.

Should her husband have encouraged and built her up? Absolutely. But she also has a responsibility to love herself.

Having broken free from an abusive relationship, I know firsthand the trauma it inflicts on the heart and emotions. But I also know - God is able to heal even the deepest wounds and make us whole if we allow Him to.

He can restore our sense of self-love, self-value, and self-worth by any means necessary - through prayer, His Word, a loving support system, and counseling.

So let me say this:
Don't lose the wonderfully and fearfully made woman God created you to be.

Self-awareness and
discernment are
your allies.
Don't ignore the
cautionary flags.
Their presence
signals potential
danger zones.

The Little Foxes

It's the little foxes that destroy the vine.
It starts off with small bites,
nibbles around the edges.
We don't pay it much attention
because the initial effects seem minuscule.

But when left unchecked,
those little foxes become huge problems -
Eating away at the vine
until there's nothing left.

Oh, we're quick to call out the obvious -
and point fingers too...
But there is One who knows the heart,
who searches and examines.
God sees and knows us through and through.

And He is saying:
Beware of the little foxes.

Don't be caught unaware.
They're lurking at your door,
waiting for the opportunity
to ensnare and destroy.

The little foxes like:

Jealousy
Bitterness
Unforgiveness
Compromise
Partiality
Envy
Hatred
Gossip
Manipulation
Pretension too

Double-mindedness
Doubt
Disbelief
Exaggeration (embellishment of the truth)

Pride
Arrogance
Fear
Selfishness
Self-righteousness
Impatience
Denial

...Just to name a few.

All of these - and more - only come to tear down
and divide.
Keep them away from your house:
Your marriage
Your family
Your church too.

Submit to God.
Resist the devil -
and he will flee from you.

Be quick to go to God
and cry out for help at the first sign.
Don't live in denial.
Refuse to allow the little foxes
to destroy the vine.

The Other Forbidden Fruit

When God told Adam
Not to eat from the Tree of the Knowledge
of Good and Evil,
He did so knowing that if Adam
ate of the forbidden fruit,
it would mean certain death.

Yet Adam and Eve ate the fruit anyway -
and sin entered the world...

The Song of Solomon speaks of
another forbidden fruit -
what I call Premature Love.

I hear the warnings come through the writer's pen:
Don't stir up love till it pleases.
Don't stir up love till it pleases.
Don't stir up love till it pleases.

Be on guard.
Guard your heart.
Stabilize your emotions.
Control your passion.

Love stirred up too soon can wound the heart.

May be the right person.
Even the right place...
But God is saying:
Not the right time.
Wait.

I'm still preparing.
Not ready yet.
Not free to love.
Still need to let go of the old.

Can't love you the way
you deserve to be loved right now.
A day is coming...
just not this day.

Wait, I say.
Love can't please right now.
Only heartache awaits.

Listen to Me.
Heed the warning.
Don't eat of the other forbidden fruit.

Don't stir up love till it pleases.

It won't always be this way.
Just need you to trust and obey.

51

There is a set time -
when love will please.
Freely flowing from heart to heart –

Mutually expressed,

An articulation of vows

Rehearsed in the hearing of witnesses -
   Written upon the heart.

Receiving and returning,

Intimacy heightened and deepened,

Adoration and love -

Gifts to one another:
   You to me. Me to you.

Endorsed, joined, and sealed by God.

This is My promise.
My covenant to you -
when you wait,
instead of partaking of the other forbidden fruit.

Don't stir up love till it pleases.

Girlfriend on The Inside

You say you're bored
with the way things are.
Just not the same for you.
Something has changed -
and of course,
you say that change is not you.

You are still the same,
So you say.
You haven't changed,
So you say.
You just don't feel
the way you used to.

You need someone you can talk to,
relate to -
So you say.
You need someone who can excite you,
tantalize you -
So you say.

Why do some think the grass is greener
on the other side?
That the girlfriend -
Yeah, the girlfriend on the outside -

is the answer?

When all that you need
is the Girlfriend inside the Wife
you left on the inside.

Did you forget
that your wife is your girlfriend too?

What happened to you
stirring the pot,
keeping the flames of passion
alive and burning hot?

When you saw her losing herself in you,
did you tell her:

She's beautiful?
She has value?
She has worth?

Did you encourage her?
Did you build her up?
Or did you take pleasure in her neglect of self,
because being her world
stroked your ego?

You say things have changed...

But what did you do
to maintain the Girlfriend inside the Wife
on the inside?

But that's alright.

I'm awake now.
Awake to God's love for me.
Awake to self-love.
Self-value.
Self-worth.

No more neglecting me.
No more loving you
more than I love me.
No more walking with my head down.

I am more than just "somebody."
I am the King's daughter -
Royalty.

You wanted a girlfriend?
Take a good look at me, baby.

Because the girlfriend on the outside
don't even come close to comparing
to the Girlfriend inside the Wife
on the inside.

Take a good look at my stature and curves -
I know I look fine.
Take a good look at my eyes -
I know you're mesmerized.

Trying to figure out what has taken place.
Cause what you thought was dead and gone -
God has resurrected by His power and grace!

I see you drooling…
You may want to close your mouth
before you wet up your clothes.

Do you need a bib, baby?
I got you.

You see God blessing.
You see God prospering -
despite the lies told.

Now the girlfriend on the outside
is losing her appeal.

You have been awakened
to the Girlfriend inside the Wife
you left on the inside.

Wolf in Sheep's Clothing

Piercing eyes
Chocolate surprise
Six-pack abs
Ripped to a T
The perfect picture -
if the focus is purely externalities...

Charismatic
Debonair
Comedic relief
You know the right words -
Like liquid gold they flow from your lips:
Enticing
Flattering
Bait for unsuspecting prey.

A wolf in sheep's clothing
coming to play.

You seek and look,
confident in your plan.

Character
Integrity
Heart

Honesty
Accountability -
What are these?

None are required at your hand.

Time has proven:
Good looks and manipulation are enough to
withstand.

"Give her a little fine and funny" is your motto -
And you'll have her eating out of your hands...

Not so!

My Daddy ain't raised me to be no fool.
He's told me 'bout your kind -
The wolf in sheep's clothing
whose aim is to trap and devour.

He's taught me to look beyond the surface
and examine the man beneath -
His words,
Actions,
Walk,
Life -
What does it speak?

He's given me examples in His Word
of how a man should be…
The standard has been set -
either you will measure up
or flee.

Can't go back.
He's opened my eyes
to discern and see…

**Nothing is off
limits with God.
He desires to lead
you in every area of
life, including
matters of
the heart.
Yes, even in
romance…**

Unlikely Love Affair

FAITH & ROMANCE

Many waters cannot quench love, neither can floods drown it.

Song of Solomon 8:7

[2]Faith is defined as:

1. *Complete trust or confidence in someone or something.*
2. Hebrews 11:1 – *"Now faith is the substance of things hoped for, the evidence of things not seen."*

Romance is defined as:

1. *A love affair.*
2. *Ardent emotional attachment or involvement between people; love.*
3. *To make love; to court, to woo.*

At first glance, faith and romance may seem like an unlikely pair.

But can true romance exist without faith?
I believe the answer is no.

The very essence of romance assumes that the love shown will be received and returned in some form by the other person. Very few couples enter into a lifelong covenant of marriage without some level of

---

[2] Definitions for "faith" and "romance" - Dictionary.com

trust and confidence in the one they're choosing to build a life with.

From the first meeting, to the friendship, to the first date, to the courtship, to the proposal, to marriage and beyond - each step requires faith.

To woo and pursue someone in love requires faith.

You need a measure of confidence that you can win their heart and capture their love and affection for a lifetime.

To share intimacy with your spouse requires faith.

You must believe that when you come together, both of you will experience mutual fulfillment – a loving exchange of vulnerability, affection, and trust.

To maintain and grow in love over time requires faith.

You're believing that the love between you will not fade but deepen. That it will mature, becoming stronger and sweeter through life's seasons.

While some of us may define romance differently, most of us carry the hope and expectation that the love we give will be reciprocated. That some sort of exchange will take place in response to our love.

So, when you really think about it, the union between faith and romance is not strange at all. In fact, they go hand in hand.

The "unlikely love affair" isn't so unlikely after all...

The Faith Walk

"Life is a box of chocolates."
I remember this quote from the movie,
Forrest Gump.
Simply put, you never know what life
will bring your way.
and because of that, we need faith...

A life without faith is a life without victory!

Faith forces one to look beyond what he or she sees.
Faith compels one to believe God for better.
Faith demands one to take courage,
Instead of giving in to fear.

Faith causes you to step out into the unknown
and trust God to navigate the course as you go.

Faith exercises restraint
and doesn't **in-ter-fere** *(enter fear)*
to try and help God along.

Faith pleases God.
No one can come to God unless you have faith to
believe He is…

Faith silences doubt and embraces God's Word.
Faith is evidence of the unseen hope.
Faith manifests the promises of God.

Everything in life requires faith -
The ability, wherewithal, gusto, determined resolve
to confidently believe God in and for all things that
concern us...

Including LOVE.

Yes - LOVE.

Who better to invite into your love journey than God? He knows you and your future spouse better than anyone else, and He desires the very best for you.

Romance isn't just about falling in love. It's about believing that love is worth the risk.

The Connection

You always seemed out of my reach…
Just didn't think I was your type of woman -
It's not that I thought myself to be lesser than,
Just didn't see how I fit you.

I found myself pondering how…
Now that I had taken notice of you.

We really didn't have much interaction.
Didn't mingle in the same circles
or share common friends.

I was this introvert -
A quiet woman who stayed to herself.
And you - this engaging man
who others sought to be around.

Only God knew
That our worlds would eventually collide.

And collide they did -
Not with a shower of fireworks,
Or the bang of bass drums,
Or the roaring of ocean waves...

But in the power of an embrace.

Not one fueled by physical attraction -
The Spirit drove this connection.

I wondered…
God, what is this?
What are You doing?

As I didn't have the words
to describe what I was feeling.

All I knew
was that a connection had occurred.

The whys and hows and whens of the connection
surpassed me…

For reasons only known to God,
He chose to connect us in a way
That transcends the natural -
Spirit to Spirit.

The Connection.

It was unexpected.
It was divine.

This Gots to Be Real

Is this real or memorex?
God, I don't understand what has taken place -
I just know what I am feeling.
I have never felt for anyone since…

All these years
and suddenly I'm awakened to love again.

I'm careful not to be presumptuous.
Don't want to read more into this than I should
or allow my emotions to override common sense.
But I can't shake what I'm feeling.

I know what it is to like,
to even lust.
But this is different.
This is LOVE…

This gots to be real.
The love I feel -
not memorex at all.
This is definitely the real deal.

Don't know when or how it happened…
It just did… and it's wonderful.
Can't explain.

No need for questions.
Don't have any answers…
It is what it is!

When friendship begins to feel like more…

The Transition

When did I make the transition
from platonic to romantic love?
Yes, I see you.
And yes, there is a connection.
But we've yet to have a first date…
We're just friends… right?

Gots to be real.
I'm fully awake to this new feeling,
but apprehensive too -
not sure if you are feeling me
like I'm feeling you.

I saw this coming.
Should've put the brakes on before it got here…
But it was just too easy
to share my heart with you.

There was a liberty with you
that I've never experienced with any other person.
I felt safe with you -
that I could trust you.

For you, too, opened up your heart
and shared with me.

We say "I love you,"
and we do.

It's just that…
the way I'm loving you now
is more than as a friend.

So how do you maintain a friendship
when your heart has moved past that point
and desires more?

How do you continue to laugh and talk
and joke around with the friend
who has now become a focus of your affection?

If I back away, he may ask, "Why?"
That'll give me a chance to open up
and express what I'm really feeling.

And I'm actually free enough with him
to do exactly that -
just not sure if that's the right thing to do.

But can I continue on
as if nothing has changed?

Will you notice the look in my eyes?
Will you sense the shift,

although I'm doing my best
to keep what I'm feeling from showing?

I just don't want to run the risk
of ruining the friendship -
if my being honest now
makes you feel awkward around me...

But the thing is,
I'm already feeling awkward!!!

And that, in and of itself,
will eventually affect us too.

The transition for me
has already occurred.

I can't pretend that it hasn't.

So, I choose to be honest
with the man I've always been able
to be open and honest with.

Plus, neither of us is dating -
just maybe... this is the reason why.

I go with my heart guarded,
knowing that he may not feel the same way.

I just need to release - no strings attached -
from one heart to another
regarding this transition.

And I'm willing to accept
the outcome of my decision…
whatever that may be.

**Sometimes the loudest
moments come without
a sound.**

Silence

You could hear a pin needle drop,
That's how quiet it was in the room.

The air was thick with silence.
I could hear his mind turning -
Contemplating,
Reflecting,
Trying to see how best to respond to me.

I just told him about the transition -
Probably the hardest conversation
I've ever had with him.

But at the same time,
It felt like a weight
was lifted off my shoulders.

We always pride ourselves on open communication.
This was definitely a test of that.

Silence, still.

He looks at me intently -
as if looking into me.

What is he trying to figure out?
What is he thinking?

The time is prolonged -
Not really,
Haven't even been one minute… Lol.
Just feels like forever.

Just say something,
I'm thinking to myself.

Silence, still.

Then, I feel his hand touch mine...
And his other hand gently caress
The side of my face.

Then that mesmerizing smile…
Yeap, that's the smile.

And of course,
I smile too -
It's infectious.
Always has been.

And he looks
And says…

Between the question and the reply lives the courage to love.

The Response

I love you too.
I have so longed to take our relationship
to the next level
and move to a place of intimacy with you.

To be honest,
We moved beyond the point of friendship some
time ago.
Why we never addressed it until now, God knows.
Maybe it was just a matter of timing…

Because we were friends,
I wasn't sure how to make the transition
to ask for more.

Call it a case of nerves -
Actually, let me be honest…
More of a fear of being rejected.
Yes, men fear rejection too.

I knew you loved me,
Just wasn't sure how you loved me.
So I decided to play it safe
and say nothing.

But saying nothing was becoming harder to do.
My poker face -
increasingly impossible to maintain.

I too wanted more.

So when you opened up to me…
All I could say within myself,
For those first few moments, was:

"Wow… thank you God."

Then, some other thoughts crossed my mind,
But it was best that I didn't act on them…

The woman I loved and desired with all my heart
Just told me she was in love with me too -
and I couldn't say a word.

I'll just wave my hand… Lol
(Okay, went old school for a moment - bringing it
back in.)

For real,
I was held in silent wonder.

But then I heard God say,
"She's waiting on you."

Then I just looked at you…
and it took all the God in me
to keep from grabbing you
in a passionate embrace and kiss.

Got to maintain self-control.
(Fast and pray, fast and pray!)

Woman - you have me!!

So here we are…
Tried so hard to hide the way we feel… Lol

Okay, for real -
You with me, baby?
We're out now -
No going back.
Only moving forward from here.

Forward to the more
That God has for us…

"What's that buzzing sound?"
I awake to my alarm clock going off -
It was all a dream.

The silence,
The response…

As the reality of the moment sets in, I muse…

The transition… Do or Don't?
My mind was made up -
Until the ALARM went off…

We've been friends -
How many years now?

We've shared, talked, laughed,
and shed tears together -

If he wanted more than friendship,
why wouldn't he express it?

I understand that men have fears too, but…
He knows me.
He's not dealing with a stranger -
I'm his friend…

What was once a whisper in prayer is now a knock at the door.

Destiny Rings

Who's at my door this time of the morning?
It's only 8:30 AM.

I look out the window and see his car.
This is unexpected...
Why is he here?

You see, we jog most Saturdays together.
We generally carpool,
But decided earlier in the week
to just meet up at the park.

I yell from upstairs, *"I'm coming,"*
and proceed to the door.

"Hey... didn't expect to see you till later."
(I say in my inquisitive voice)

As I look, there's something different about him.
He seems so serious.
"Are you alright?" I ask.

He smiles,
"Are you going to let me in?"

"Oh," I step aside to let him in.

Closing the door behind him,
I notice something in his hand.

"What's that?"

You remember when we first met…
You hardly said a word to me.
You weren't impressed with my looks or position -
Most do take a second look,
But not you...

I found myself observing, watching you.
You intrigued me.
You were just so different...

Your quietness,
Meekness -
You were beautiful inside and out…
and still are.

I knew you were the one then,
But I wasn't ready.
Too many unresolved issues and unhealed hurts.
I needed healing.

Then we connected

and became friends.

Our friendship was perfect -
It kept you close to me
without commitment.

Selfish, I know.

God wouldn't allow me to continue in that state -
I had to confront the pain of my past,
So I could heal and move forward.

I opened my heart to you
because I felt safe with you.
You listened without casting judgment.
You actually heard me -

Yet, I remained afraid…

But then I felt a shift in you.
There was this awkwardness,
A pulling away
that I didn't understand...
"Were you leaving me too?"

Our friendship as I knew it
was changing.

I knew I didn't want to lose you -
I love you.

I had a choice to make:
Embrace love
or lose out because of fear.

Love won.

Before you say anything,
Please read this…

He handed over the note
That he was holding in his hand.

By now, I was speechless.
No jogging today.

I settled into the corner of my sofa
and began to read…

The note that changed everything.

The Man Beneath the Beautiful Speaks

Beautiful exterior
Pleasing to the eye
Onlookers admire
As I walk by

Never too close
Walls to guard
Smiles to hide…
The fear to love -
To let that one inside

The war wages behind the eyes
The mind wrestles:
Fear vs. Love

The one - I like
The one - I love
The one - I desire and need
Truly believe:
My gift from God above

But fear keeps me at bay
Instead of reaching and receiving
I turn away

I want to embrace
I want to receive so badly that it hurts

How do I let go of the fear?
Break down the walls that have kept me
safe?
So I thought…

Now the one is here and near
So close, but still…

God says:
Perfect love casts out fear.

He was right!

Never thought I'd love like this again -
Could open up my heart to anyone else
like this again,

But God has perfected me in His love
that -
Subdues all fears
Crumbles all my walls
Lets me smile for real.

Not hiding.
Not pushing away.

The man beneath the beautiful
is now open
For the one to see -
To know
To touch
To love
To become one with me.

**God restored
what fear
tried to bury.
Now love
has nothing
to withhold.**

Withholding Nothing

With tears streaming down my face,
I look at him and ask,

"What does this mean?"

I knew doggone well
(as my granddaddy would say)
what he meant;
I just wanted him to say it!

He comes over
and kneels in front of me.

He gently lifts my chin,
so I can see directly into his eyes, and
says -

"I love you."

The note - it means that I'm ready:
Ready to receive and unwrap you
as my gift from God.
Ready to fully commit
without reservation or hesitation.

Ready to provide, cover,
and take care of you as God ordains.

I'm ready to love you
like you deserve to be loved -
as my wife.

Completely.
Withholding nothing.

**Only a whole heart
can give itself fully.**

Love That Pleases

WHERE HONOR & PASSION EMBRACE

> He brought me to the banqueting house, and his **banner** over me was love.
> *Song of Solomon 2:4*

If You Want Me, Then Unwrap Me

The world says,
(singing)
"If you want me, come and get me…"
Not!

(singing)
"If you want me, then receive me,
and be willing to unwrap me!"

You see, my brother -
God has given me as a gift to you…

And I can tell you are aware of who I am
from your vernacular.

You say,
"I'm God-sent."
You say,
"I'm a jewel."

But it's not enough to discern
that I am God's Gift to you.

The question is:
Do you want me?

If you want me, unwrap me.
But before you can unwrap me,
you gots to receive me.

You see, you still have the choice
to accept or decline the Gift…

Ain't forcing love, my brother.

But I see that you are a man
who knows what he wants -
and when God places the Gift
he desires in his view,
you're wise enough to receive what God's given…

Now on to the fun part – unwrapping me!

You see…

I ain't no little girl
waiting to be awakened to her prince.

I've known about you for some time.
Just had to wait for God to ready you for me.

Now it's time for discovery…
Others have looked at me
and tried to figure me out based on what they see:

Too quiet for some.
Too skinny for others.
Too spiritual to be any fun – boring, so they
assumed…

The thing with me?
I can't be read like that - on purpose.

God didn't design me to be an easy read.

But the thing is -
I was never their gift anyway.
I was yours.

You'll quickly discover, my brother,
that there's more to me than meets the eye.

Yes, I am the spiritual woman that you see -
Loving God with all my heart.

He is my source,
my rock,
the reason I am who I am today -
A woman loving life and looking forward
to sharing her life with you.
God preserved me for you.

No sampling.

No handling.
No premature unwrapping…

For your eyes only.

Now…

I'm laden with treasures
waiting to be opened by you.

God has given you the key -
use it wisely.

This gift holds quite a few surprises too…
So I hope you're excited for what awaits you!

The world says,
(singing)
"If you want me, come and get me…"
Not!

(singing)
"If you want me,
then receive me,
and be willing to unwrap me!"

And you have…!

Passion Under Control

Light
Free
Amazingly Beautiful
is the way I feel when I'm with you.

Just one look.
Just one touch.

The strength and gentleness of your embrace
Leaves me speechless -
Gasping for air.

What is this I feel, I ask?
Every part of my being responds to you!
I wonder...
Can you feel me?
Can you sense my desire for you?

Do you hear my heart racing?
Do you notice my body
quiver at the slightest touch of your hand?

Never felt this way for anyone since...
You're the first.

The passion in you
has awakened the passion in me.

But wait!
  - can't stir love till it pleases.
Not in a position to please or be pleased.
So, I wait -
Passion under control.

I must admit
you turn me on...
when you keep passion under control.

To know you are awake to me too,
But willing to wait
          and do it God's way,
Just further endears my heart to you.

I love God.
and I love you.

So, I wait for the right time -
To stir up all my love for you.
To ignite all my desire for you.
To be loosed in uncontrolled,
exhilarating passion
for you.

I wait for our wedding day -
The time that I will be joined to you.
Become completely one with you.
Bone of your bone,
Flesh of your flesh…
One!

So until then...
Passion under control.
Lord, help!

**But the fruit of
the Spirit
is love, joy, peace,
longsuffering,
kindness, goodness,
faithfulness,
gentleness,
self-control.
Against such
there is no law.**
Galatians 5:22-23

And the two will become one flesh. So they are no longer two, but one.

Mark 10:8

My Side My Rib

I came out of him and now am in him again.
He is my side and I am his rib -
Bone of my bone, flesh of my flesh,
Once twain, now one.

They say that true love between a man and a
woman is hard to find -
a rarity, one that some never experience in their
lifetime.
If this holds true, its rarity by definition
makes it that much more valuable and desirable.

And when taken hold,
you are not easily persuaded to let go
or willing to part from it.

You see…
It's something special for a man to find
and marry the woman
that perfectly fits his side,
And for the woman to answer
and embrace the man
from whose side she was suited
and adapted to fit…

More than just physical attraction
or electrifying chemistry that sizzles hot in the
beginning,
Only to wax cold in the end.

More than a momentary fix
or temporary cure to soothe the lonely soul.

More than playmates
in a partnership of convenience…
Hmm.

He has literally found his rib,
and she, her side…
WOW!

His Rib, who…
Deeply loves and enjoys him
Helps, aids, and builds him up
Compliments and adds to him
Honors and respects him
Prays for him
Submits willingly to him,
        not out of obligation, but trust and love
Is a fountain of peace and a bed of wisdom
Seeks how she may please and care for him
Is a good thing and brings favor from God.

Her Side, who…
Unites and cleaves to her
Loves her as Christ loves the Church
   completely, freely, fully—more than enough
Protects and provides for her as head
Doesn't exploit her submissiveness
but sees her as his own body
   thus cherishes and nourishes her
Complements and adds to her
Honors and respects her
Prays for her
Lives with her according to knowledge and
understanding
Seeks how he may please and care for her too.

He says, "My Rib."
She says, "My Side."

Covenant says:
My Side My Rib
One of the same body,
with shared and mutually inclusive interests.

The beauty and the value of this
is not that they are exempt from
difficulties and challenges -
but that after all is said and done,
their love and commitment to one another remains.

Now in this lies its rarity and true worth.

Those of you who have this -
don't let it go.
Those of you who desire this -
when your day arrives,
Treasure it, understanding the value
of true love and covenant.

My Side My Rib

The beauty of covenant love.

I Love

I love your smile.
I love the way you operate with compassion and
love.
I love your sense of humor.
I love the wisdom and insight God has given you.
I love your humility.
I love your love for God.

I love the way you pray for me.
I love the way you hold and embrace me.
I love the way you look at me...
    You make me feel like I'm the most beautiful
woman in the world.

I love your creativity.
I love your friendship -
    You're the first man I've felt free enough to
want to share my heart.

I love talking to you,
    listening to you,
        being with you.

I love the fact that I feel safe with you.
I LOVE you!

Ruth to Her Boaz

God gave me His best
when He joined me to you.

No turning back.
No running away.
I'm yours, and you are mine.

Where you go – I will go.
Your people will be my people.
Our God, the true and living God,
Forever God.

You have captured my heart
in a way that no other man has…
I only want you.

You got me, baby -
My heart - My love
My attention - My affection

There's no other place I'd rather be than with you.
You are my desire…
Absolutely no other man for me.

ONLY YOU!

There is a
part of me
that only you
get to see.
For your
eyes only.

You Bring Out the Flirt in Me

There's a part of my nature
that only you get to see -
For it is strictly reserved for the man,
God says is for me.
It's the flirtatious side of me.

Quiet, yes.
Boring, no.

A little shy, yes.
Cold, no.

Quite the opposite, actually…

Very passionate.
Die-hard romantic.
No other man will ever see -
Only you can bring out the flirt in me.

I know my strengths
and the effects that can ensue.
I enjoy to tease, and that's okay -
I'm in position now to please you too…

I can get you all hot and bothered - as you say -

Take you to heights in your mind with delicious
words,
caressing your soul.

The promised land,
hands gently explore:

Triggers
Hot spots
Hot springs
Sudden surges of delight

Is it here?
Or maybe there?

No need to rush…
Purposed to savor and take pleasure
in every moment that God blesses me
to share with you.
Taking no day for granted -
I'm honored to be married to you.

See what you did?
Yes you, my love.
You used your key wisely
and opened up one of the treasures within:

I'm only wired for you…

Only have eyes for you…
Only desire to be with and please you…

You see, this flirtatious side of me,
God has given ALL to you.

For Your Eyes Only!

**Let him kiss me
with the kisses of
his mouth -
for your love
is more delightful
than wine.**
Song of Solomon 1:2 NIV

Speechless

Eyes mesmerized.
Hearts racing.
Panting breaths.

Fire blazing.
Warming sensations
- melting, intertwining, manifesting.

No words.
Sounds making melody
held in speechless ecstasy.

The chambers are now closed.
Reserved for your eyes only!

The king has brought me into his chambers.

Song of Solomon 1:4

Naked and Unafraid

Here I am
Here I am
Standing naked and unafraid
Naked and unashamed.

You know what I love...
I don't have to hide from you.
I don't have to present a fictitious me -
You prefer me real, genuine, and free.

No need to cover my imperfections,
'Cause you know them all
and still love me.

My mind is at ease,
My soul is at peace.
I find rest in the security and comfort of your
embrace.

You never have to wonder where I am,
For you stand naked and unafraid with me.
You also are free to be -
untroubled, unpretentious in my presence -
a safe place to release your dreams, fears,
and vulnerabilities.

You are enough.
You are enough.
The only man for me.

We are as we should be -
Loving, being loved,
Living out love daily…
You and me
My Side My Rib
Husband and Wife
One under God's sovereign authority.

The Garden of Eden painted the perfect picture:
Two dwelling as one -
Adam and Eve.
Naked and unafraid,
Naked and unashamed.

Then sin entered…

The nakedness which God esteemed as beautiful
now caused them shame.
They ran and hid.
Instead of accountability,
they played the blame game.

Beloved, let us keep this lesson close.
Let us always honor God's Word above all else -

Lest sin enters and disrupts our flow.

Let us always be real with one another -
listening, receiving
mutual exchanges of the thoughts of the heart.

Unafraid because of our love.
Unashamed because of the trust we have shared
from the start.

Not perfect people,
Just naked -
Bare before God and each other.

Our love is worth it.
So, we choose to fight for us,
instead of against us.

And we do so:
Naked and unafraid,
Naked and unashamed.

Therefore what God has joined together, let no one separate.

Mark 10:9 NIV

Prayers in Prose

FOR MY BELOVED

Ask, and it will be given to you; seek, and you will find; knock, and it will be opened to you. For everyone who asks receives, and he who seeks finds, and to him who knocks it will be opened.
Matthew 7:7-8 NIV

You Are the One

Never in my wildest dreams
could I have imagined a better gift
than the one God has given me in you…
Beautiful man of God.

You are the one I hoped for…

God, thank You for blessing me with a man who:

- Is submitted to You
- Loves You, loves himself, and loves me as Christ loves the Church
- Is consistent in his relationship with You and faithful service
- Has a strong yet gentle character
- Is courteous, has vision, and willingly works with his hands
- Is honest and trustworthy
- Is determined and not quick to quit
- Is secure in his own uniqueness and confident in You
- Is a praying man
- Is uninhibited in his worship and praise to You.

You are the one I longed for…

Father, thank You for my beloved who:

- Respects and values me
- Invests time to know me
- Is my friend and accepts me for me
- Gives me room to grow
- Makes me laugh
- Prays for me

Thank You, Father, for this genuine man of God!

You are the one I waited for...

Thank You, Lord, for my beloved who:

- Complements and adds to me
- Cleaves to me and I to him
- Desires to please me as much as I desire to please him
- Is committed and faithful to me
- Has received me as Your gift and desires covenant with me
- Only has eyes for me - and I, for him

Thank You for my beloved who was well worth the wait!

You are my beloved, the one I prayed for...

God, keep my beloved - preserve him in integrity and uprightness as he waits on You.

- Let Your blood cover him and all You've placed in his care.
- Be his banner, protection, and grant him victory.
- Let all grace (favor and earthly blessings) come to him in abundance, so he has all he needs.
- Bless the work of his hands - cause him to flourish and succeed.
- Let him bring forth fruit in season, with leaves that do not wither;
- And let everything he puts his hands to - prosper and come to maturity
- Give him a discerning spirit and favor him with Your wisdom, knowledge, and truth
- Order his steps according to Your Word and lead him in the paths of righteousness for Your name's sake too.

Father, keep my beloved rooted and grounded in Your Word.

- Let neither Your truth nor mercy depart from him.

- But, let it be bound around his neck and written upon his heart that he remains in the way that leads to everlasting life.

Father, intensify his love walk with You.

- Bless him with the desire to always seek You first.
- Let him not be complacent in his relationship with You, but be found hungering and thirsting for more of You.
- Let the light that shines from him always point back to You, O God.
- Let him take the example of Jesus and make of himself no reputation - do Your will and stay humble before You.

Father, favor him with creativity, innovative ideas, and strategy for the vision that You have placed in his heart.

Let him know that with You all things are possible and bless him with the:

- Faith to believe
- Patience to endure and
- Conviction to stand upon Your Word

Perfect him in Your love that casts out fear.
Let him walk in the spirit of power, love, and a sound mind.

Let his mind be bound to the mind of Christ and mature him in Your perfect will.

Lord, help him to guard his heart with all diligence.
- Bless him to forgive, when needed.
- Bless him to let go, when You have purposed him to do so.
- Bless him to freely love as You have so freely given.
- And make him in every way whole.

Lord, guide him continually and
keep him from temptations too.
If he finds himself tempted, help him to resist and remain submitted to You.

Bless him with a healthy body and a long life that satisfies - enjoyable, vibrant, and abundant in You.

In the places where he may be weak, infuse and perfect Your strength in him too.
And finally, Our Father:

Let praise be ever on his lips and
worship in his heart for You, O God.
And may he continually abide and rest in Your
presence - full of peace, love, and joy.
In Jesus' Name, Amen.

You are the one I was reserved for...
For Your Eyes Only

God bless:

- Us to honor our covenant vows, so our
  marriage always honor You.
- To submit to You first, then to one another
  in all that we say and do.

Father, bless our marriage bed with intimacy,
creativity, and spice, so that we always find
satisfaction in each other's embrace.

- Flood our hearts and home with laughter and
  joy.
- Let us be quick to forgive and make up.

Let our love for each other
only become more potent
and sweeter with time –
aged in grace and unconfined.
Cement us in love;

So that when challenges arise,
they only make
our covenant stronger,
bond tighter,
resolve firmer –
to remain as one.

Father, let the channels of communication always remain open between me and my beloved.

- Let us be each other's ear and confidant.
- Sharing and upholding each other in prayer, wisdom, understanding, peace, and love.

Father bless our home, so every need is supplied. Let neither Your Word nor Your Presence depart from us.

At all times, guide us O God and bless us with longevity that we may mature to a ripe old age together – free of disease and strife.

Finally, my Father – let my beloved only have eyes for me, and I for him. Let us rest in You always and what You have sealed and joined together, let no man separate, in Jesus Name. Amen.

A Prayer of Blessing for the Wedding Day

I was asked to pray at the wedding of a dear sister and brother in the Lord, and the Lord gave me this prayer of blessing for their special day. Today, I am sharing it with you. I have removed their names so that, if the Lord wills, this blessing can be prayed at future weddings too.

Father, thank You for Your presence
that fills this room.
You have been gracious.
You have been kind.
You have been liberal in Your outpouring of love
on us and for that we say, thank You!

Thank You for this beautiful occasion
for which we have gathered today –
to witness the wedding, the coming together as one
of _____and _____.
This is Your doing, and it is marvelous in our eyes.

Now Father, as we move forward with the
consecration of this union,
let Your blessing abound in them and over them.

- The blessings of Your presence
- The blessings of Your acceptance -
  for they are accepted in the beloved
- The blessings of unity
- The blessings of peace
- The blessings of wisdom and understanding
- The blessings of honor and mutual respect
- The blessings of laughter, joy, favor, and
  intimacy
- The blessings of good health and longevity

And with their hearts turned towards You, O God
sealed them in love –
in Your love and the love You have given one for
another.

Let the vows they speak
be written upon the tablets of their hearts
as a memorial –
a daily reminder of this day
and commitment made to one another.

And in it and through it all, O God -
be the cement that binds and holds them together,
now and forever.

In Jesus' name we pray and
ascribe glory to You, O God.
Amen.

Unchanging Love. Unfailing Love. Forever reigning Love. *Made Possible Because…* **God Is Love.**

Epilogue

A LOVE WORTH TALKING ABOUT

> The Lord appeared to us in the past, saying:
> "I have loved you with an everlasting love;
> I have drawn you with unfailing kindness.
> *Jeremiah 31:3 NIV*

Regardless of our marital status, we all have the opportunity to enter into a love relationship with God. His love surpasses all others - it is everlasting, unchanging, and unconditional. God's love always was and always will be - it's just that we had to become aware of His love in order to receive it.

For some of us, that awareness required awakening from ideologies that portrayed God as distant and impersonal. Others had to work through past hurts and disappointments for which we may have blamed God. Still, some of us had to look beyond our own feelings of unworthiness to receive such love.

Yet, the first true lover of our souls is God. Our very existence evoked His love.

Just consider this: He loved us so much that, rather than leave us to waste away in our sins, He provided a remedy. Through that remedy, all of humanity has the opportunity to be saved - that is, to repent, be set free, delivered from the penalty of sin, and reconciled into a love relationship with Him. The entire story of salvation is rooted and grounded in love.

God drew us by His love. (Jeremiah 31:3)

He presented a remedy for our sins because of love. (John 3:16)

And now, through His power, we can live according to His Word in love. (Matthew 22:37–39)

So while you're waiting on your one, lean into The One who loved you first and will always love you most. His love is always present and ready to embrace you.

The best decision I've ever made was to receive God's love. My ability to give and receive love is all because of His love - a love truly worth talking about.

Though the mountains be shaken and the hills be removed, yet my unfailing love for you will not be shaken nor my covenant of peace be removed," says the Lord, who has compassion on you.

Isaiah 54:10 NIV

I am God's beloved.
I am whole, healed, and worthy of a love that reflects His heart.

I trust His timing and rest in His promises. Whether waiting, discovering, or growing in love - I walk by faith, not fear.

I am a Gift.
And I am deeply, undeniably loved.

Affirmations While I Wait

Waiting | Hoping | Growing

- ♥ I am deeply loved by God - completely, unconditionally, eternally.
- ♥ I am not forgotten. I am seen, chosen, and held in perfect love.
- ♥ While I wait, I do not wither. I worship, grow, and flourish in faith.
- ♥ God is preparing me and the one He has for me, in His perfect time.
- ♥ I hold fast to faith, knowing that what God promises, He fulfills.
- ♥ I release fear, doubt, comparison, and receive healing.
- ♥ I am whole and free to love again.
- ♥ Love will find me whole, ready, and deeply anchored in God.
- ♥ I trust God's hand in my story, even when I don't see the next chapter.
- ♥ My heart is safe in His timing.
- ♥ My steps are ordered, even in the waiting.
- ♥ My heart is guarded by wisdom and open through discernment.
- ♥ Love is not something I chase - it's something I receive in peace.

- The delays are not denials - they are divine preparation.
- I can desire love while still being content in God.
- I am worth knowing, worth pursuing, and worth loving well.
- I do not settle. I wait with hope, because I believe in covenant love.
- Every lesson, every healing moment, is making room for a deeper love.
- I am God's gift, wrapped in wisdom, grace, and purpose.
- My love story is in the hands of the One who writes the best endings.

My love story is still unfolding...

For I know the plans I have for you," declares the **Lord, "plans to prosper you and not to harm you, plans to give you hope and a future.**

Jeremiah 29:11 NIV

CONTACT AUTHOR

We'd Love to Hear from You

If *For Your Eyes Only* has blessed or inspired you in any way, we invite you to share your testimony. Your story could be the encouragement someone else needs on their journey.

You can follow Lanetta Allen on social media or connect with her through her author page at:

Because There's More Publishing
Scan the QR code or visit:
becausetheresmorepublishing.com

More books are on the way! Stay connected for future releases, updates, and inspiring content from Lanetta Allen and BTMP.